A Mystery Picture Book

Where's My Hat?

Written by Neil and Ting Morris
Illustrated by Anna Clarke

Hodder and Stoughton
London Sydney Auckland Toronto

Emma and Sam have been saving up their pocket money for weeks. There are so many things to buy at the market – it's difficult to choose! Sam would like a cowboy hat, but they are all much too big for him. Emma thinks a hat is a good idea, and so she tries on lots of different kinds. Eventually she decides on a straw hat with a long red ribbon.

Find the mystery objects:

beads

crate

belt

dog

button

lettuce

cotton reel

nail

crab

umbrella

Emma is very pleased with her new hat. And Sam is glad that he didn't spend his money – now he'll be able to afford a giant ice cream later. But first they go to the playground in the park. There they see their friends Chen and Katy, who have been playing all morning. Emma and Sam go straight on the swings, and Emma goes so high that her hat blows off in the wind.

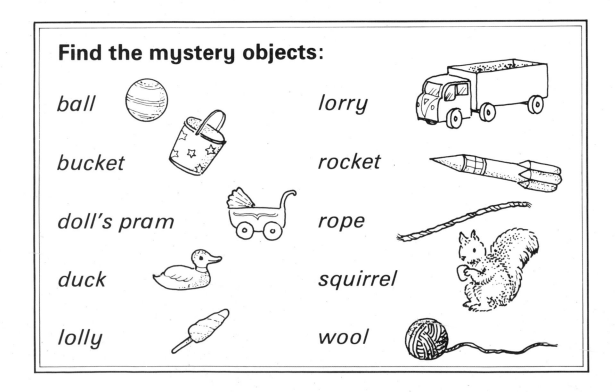

Find the mystery objects:

ball

bucket

doll's pram

duck

lolly

lorry

rocket

rope

squirrel

wool

When Emma gets off the swing, she can't find her hat anywhere! Sam helps her search all over the playground, but it's not there. 'Someone must have stolen it!' says Sam in a loud whisper. 'Don't be so silly!' says Emma. 'Thieves take jewels and money, not hats.' But secretly she thinks that Sam could be right. They run across the park together and look everywhere. Suddenly Emma catches a glimpse of her hat, but she is too late to see who is wearing it.

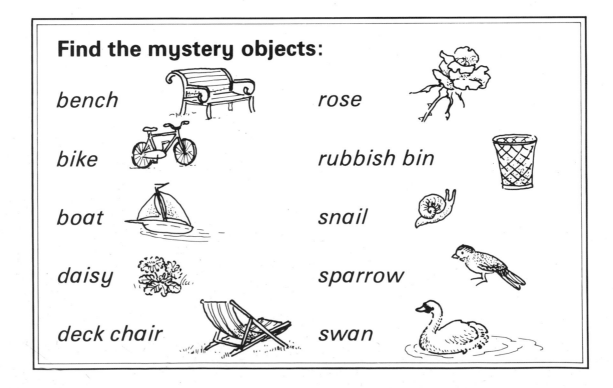

Find the mystery objects:

bench

bike

boat

daisy

deck chair

rose

rubbish bin

snail

sparrow

swan

Emma races over to where she saw the hat, and Sam does his best to keep up with her. He has never seen his sister run so fast before. 'Now I know how you can win the next school race,' says Sam. 'Just make sure you lose your hat first!' 'Don't talk so much and keep looking,' replies Emma, as Sam looks at the cakes in a shop window. 'I can see him!' she shouts suddenly. 'Come on, Sam, after that thief!' But as she speaks, the hat disappears again.

Find the mystery objects:

boot	newspaper
bread	pigeon
bus	puddle
chimney	statue
flag	walking stick

They follow the hat into a museum, where there are lots of statues and paintings. And lots of people wearing hats! But they can't see the thief, even though they know he must be there. They quickly decide to split up and go different ways round the museum, agreeing to meet at the same spot later. They still can't find the thief and Sam is so interested in the prehistoric animals that he forgets all about Emma and her hat.

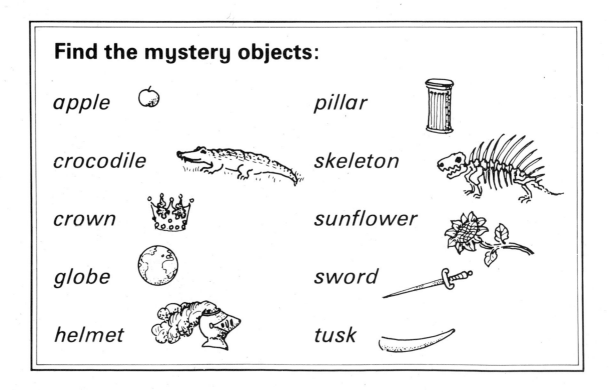

Find the mystery objects:

apple

pillar

crocodile

skeleton

crown

sunflower

globe

sword

helmet

tusk

Emma tells her brother that they had better stick together from now on. But when they leave the museum they feel like giving up the search for the hat and whoever is wearing it. Then they suddenly spot a long red ribbon disappearing into a crowd of shoppers.

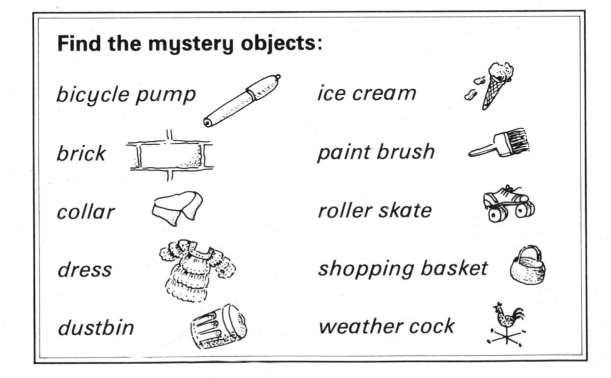

Find the mystery objects:

bicycle pump

ice cream

brick

paint brush

collar

roller skate

dress

shopping basket

dustbin

weather cock

They push their way through the crowd and find themselves inside a large store. They catch a glimpse of the thief going up an escalator, and so they jump on too. Then he goes up another escalator, and another! Emma and Sam go exactly where he goes, and they end up in the clothes department. 'Now we've lost him,' says Emma in a disappointed voice. 'Oh look, there's the hat shop over there,' says Sam. 'And there's my hat!' cries Emma. 'Come on!'

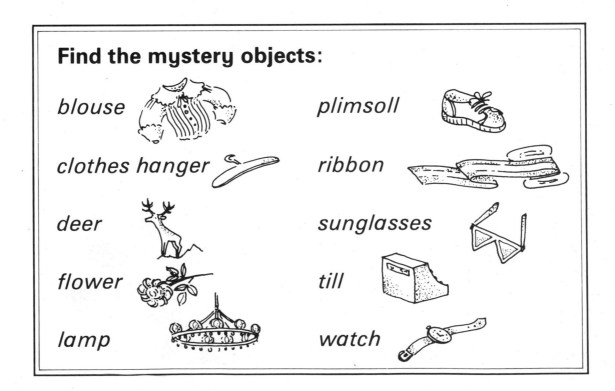

Find the mystery objects:

blouse

plimsoll

clothes hanger

ribbon

deer

sunglasses

flower

till

lamp

watch

When they get over to the hat department, they know at once that they have been tricked. 'Chen, it's you!' shouts Emma, as she recognizes him. He is standing there, pretending to be a model and hoping that they won't notice him. 'So it was you we've been chasing all the time!'

Find the mystery objects:

badge

balloon

bobble hat

cherry

feather

glove

handbag

hat stand

mirror

wig

They go and sit down in the snack bar. Emma decides it's best to keep her hat on this time, and Chen tries to explain himself. 'Well, I saw your hat blow off, and I just thought it would be fun to run off with it. I thought you would see it was me and have a game of chase. When I realized you hadn't seen me, I got quite worried. I thought you might go to the police!' 'Oh well, there's no harm done,' replies Emma. 'And we'd forgive you if only you'd get us a hamburger, wouldn't we, Sam? Chen rushes over to the counter as fast as he can . . .

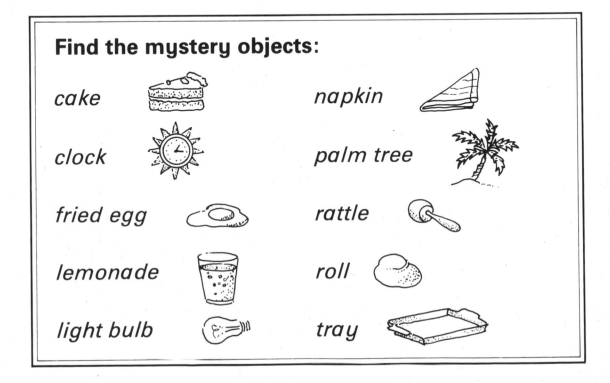

Find the mystery objects:

cake

clock

fried egg

lemonade

light bulb

napkin

palm tree

rattle

roll

tray